ZONDERVAN®

Psalm 23

Copyright © 2008 by Zondervan

Illustrations © 2008 by Barry Moser

Requests for information should be addressed to:
Grand Rapids, Michigan 49530

Library of Congress Cataloging-in-Publication Data
Moser, Barry.
 Library of Congress
 Psalm 23 / illustrated by Barry Moser.
   p. cm. -- (The master illustrator series)
 ISBN-13: 978-0-310-71085-1 (hardcover)
 ISBN-10: 0-310-71085-5 (hardcover)
 1. Bible. O.T. Psalm XXIII--Juvenile literature. I. Title. II. Title: Psalm 23.
 BS145023rd 2006
 223'.20520814--dc22

                            2006027616

Editors: Bruce Nuffer and Betsy Flikkema
Art direction: Barry Moser and Joy Chu
Cover design: Barry Moser and Laura Maitner-Mason

Printed in China

08 09 10 11 12 • 10 9 8 7 6 5 4 3 2 1

Barry Moser

PSALM 23

Dear Reader,

I hope that as you look at the pictures that I have done to accompany the Twenty-third Psalm, one of the great poems of all time, you will think it is an unusual setting. And if you do, it will make me happy. Let me tell you why.

First, I do not like doing things that a reader might expect. I want you, the reader, to read this well-known psalm—or any other well-known story or poem that I illustrate—and think about it in a new and unfamiliar way. If I set the psalm in the Holy Land, if I show you people of that ancient area in their traditional costumes, or if I show you shepherds tending to animals that are commonplace to you, then I take you nowhere that you haven't been before—in your imagination, in other books like this one, or in church or Sunday school literature.

Second, it is because I frequently travel in the Caribbean and have for the past thirty years. Though I spend most of my time reading and relaxing on the beach when I visit the Caribbean, I have spent a good bit of time exploring these marvelous places by car and on foot.

On some of the islands, like Antigua and Nevis, I am always struck by the abundance of goats and sheep (and wild horses too, on

Vieques) that roam and graze freely. These are not the wooly, white kinds of sheep or goats we usually think of, but lean, mostly short-haired animals of all shades and patterns of brown, black, gray, and white. You can tell the goats from the sheep only by the way they carry their tails: sheep carry their tails down, and goats carry them up. They stand, meander lazily, graze at wisps of greenery growing in cracks in the pavement, and lie down in the road. Sometimes we have no choice but to stop our car and wait for them to get on their way. You cannot hurry them because they are on "island time," as it is said, and they will just ignore you if you try. It's best to stop and wait.

Watching them, I often find myself quietly reciting the Twenty-third Psalm. How very accurate, it seems to me, is the image of the Creator watching over you and me like we were sheep. The Creator is represented here in two ways: First, and most obviously, as the shepherd, and secondly, through symbolic images. If you look closely at the pictures, you will find all sorts of symbols of God, Christ, and the Holy Spirit: doves, butterflies, and even the pelican. Maybe you can find more. They're there.

This psalm, like all the psalms, speaks to all people of all times; not just the Hebrew people from whom the Bible comes and not only in the ancient past. The psalms are yours. The psalms are mine. They are works of art—works of great and lasting beauty. And they belong to all of us, no matter what color our skin is, what era we live in, what country we inhabit, or what creed or religion we subscribe to. My favorite psalm, the one I memorized when I was a youngster like you, is this one, the Twenty-third.

Barry Moser

The LORD is my shepherd,
I shall not be in want.

He makes me lie down in green pastures,
he leads me beside quiet waters.

He restores my soul.

He guides me in paths of righteousness for his name's sake.

Even though I walk through the valley of the shadow of death, I will fear no evil.

For you are with me;
your rod and your staff,
they comfort me.

You prepare a table before me
in the presence of my enemies.

You anoint my head with oil;
my cup overflows.

Surely goodness and love will
follow me all the days of my life.

And I will dwell in the house of the LORD forever.

Note from the Publisher

Dear Reader,

The words of this book come directly from the Bible. When we think about the Bible, we think of it as a book. It has two covers and a certain set of stories within it. Of course it's a special book. One of the truly special things about it is that these stories didn't stop happening when the books of the Bible were collected in the form we know today. God kept working in his creation from that time even until today.

If you could trace all the people in the Bible through their descendents right up until today you would find that these people are your ancestors, no matter where you live or what culture you belong to. The stories and words of the Bible are not just any old stories, they are OUR stories—the words of our spiritual ancestors. What you hold in your hands is not just a picture book of ancient words, it is part of your story, and thus part of you.

So while we hope you enjoy this book, our goal is really that you will hear these words as words spoken to you from a distant relative, as meaningful today as they were the day they were written.

Sincerely,

Zondervan

This book is dedicated to my dear friends
Linford Detweiler and Karin Bergquist.

OVER THE RHINE

The artist would like to thank Akimba Thomas from Willikes Village, Antigua, West Indies, who posed for the shepherd; his mother and father, Mr. and Mrs Neal Thomas, who facilitated his participation; Mr Kenneth Charles, our dear friend who drove us around Antigua looking for sheep, goats and island scenes; the staff and management of the Long Bay Hotel, Long Bay, Antigua, who helped arrange our model and our day trip and who provided us with rest, shade, food, and warm companionship.